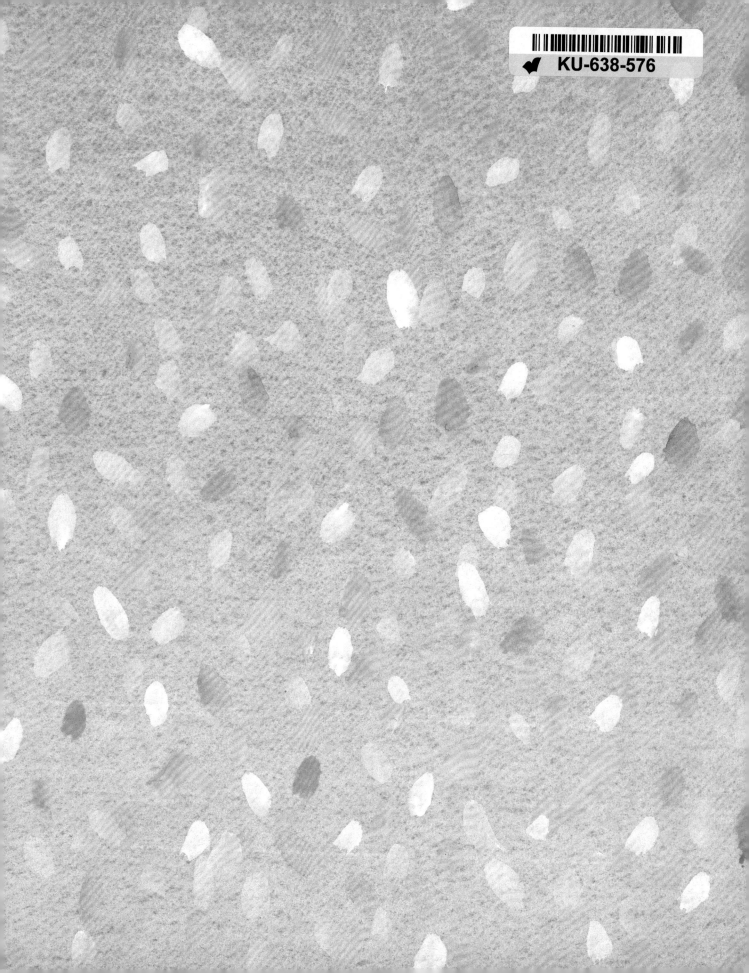

For Megan and Kerry. With thanks to Ben and Tom.
J.R.

For Tim Morris, Isaiah, Thea and Silas, who all love the snow
T.B.

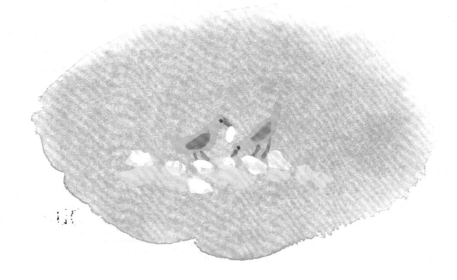

First published in Great Britain in 2009 by Gullane Children's Books
This paperback edition published 2010 by
Gullane Children's Books
185 Fleet Street, London, EC4A 2HS
www.gullanebooks.com

1   3   5   7   9   10   8   6   4   2

Text © Julia Rawlinson 2009
Illustrations © Tiphanie Beeke 2009

The right of Julia Rawlinson and Tiphanie Beeke to be identified as the author and illustrator of this work
has been asserted by them in accordance with the Copyright, Designs and Patents Act, 1988.
A CIP record for this title is available from the British Library.

ISBN: 978-1-86233-776-3

Printed and bound in China

This book belongs to

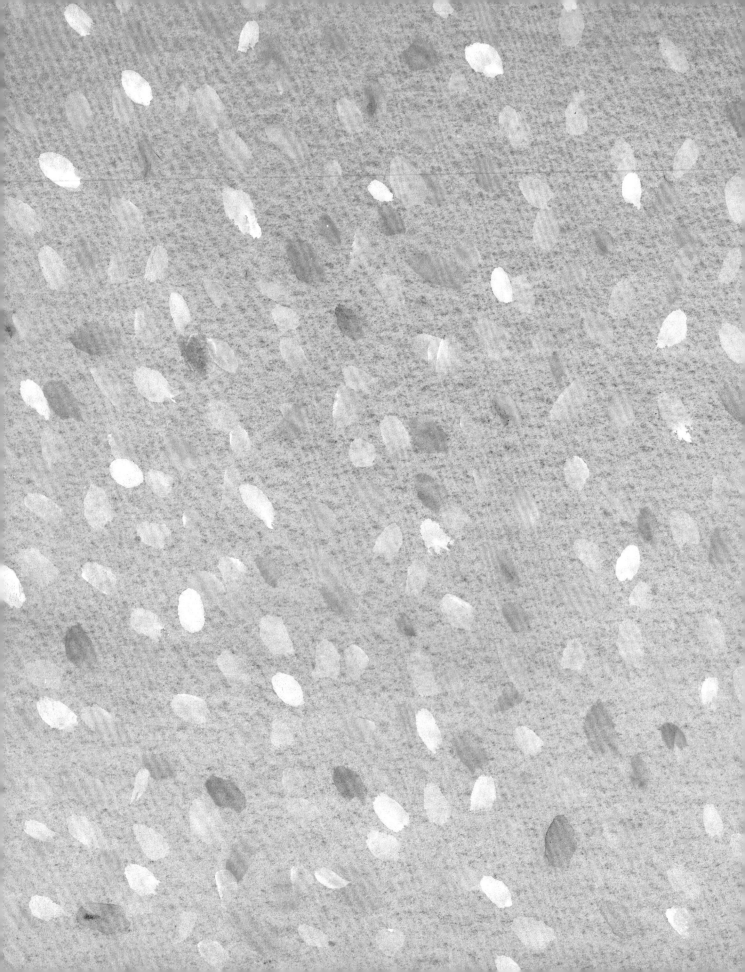

Ferdie's Springtime Blossom

Julia Rawlinson • Tiphanie Beeke

GULLANE
CHILDREN'S BOOKS

The wood was full of the
chirruping, bustling, sing-song sounds
of spring. Ferdie bounced along with his
nose in the air, sniffing the just-burst buds
of flowers and playing chase with butterflies.
With his head spinning with sights
and sounds he…

. . . tumbled happily down the hill into the sunny orchard. But when he picked himself up from the ground he couldn't believe his eyes.

Instead of the bright, rich green of spring, the
ground was covered in drifts of white, and when a soft breeze
danced through the branches it carried snowy flakes.

"Snow so late in spring," thought Ferdie. "It's much too cold
for the buds and butterflies. There's no time to lose."

He trotted busily back up the hill, wondering who he should tell, and passed a pair of doves coo-cooing on a branch.

"You've flown back to your summer home too soon," Ferdie cried.
"I've been down to the orchard and there's more snow on the way."
"Then we should fly back south," they called, "but first we
must tell Hedgehog. He's just come out of his bed of leaves.
He needs to snuggle back down or he'll freeze."

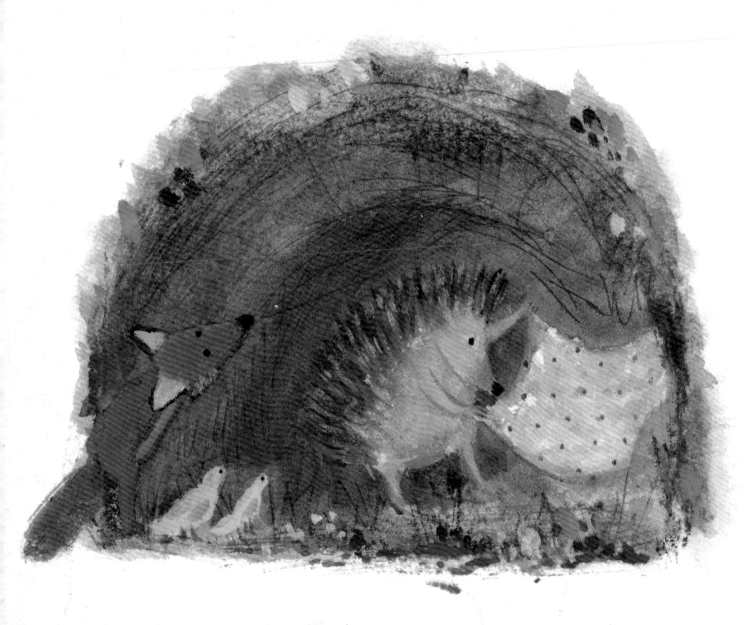

Ferdie and the doves found Hedgehog
stretching and scritch-scratching.
"There's snow on the way," panted Ferdie.
"I saw it in the orchard. It will be too cold for
the butterflies, and the doves will need to
fly south and you must hide away."

"Then I should crawl back into my bed," snuffled Hedgehog, sadly, "but first we must tell Squirrel that he needs to hunt for food. He's eaten all his winter store of nuts. He'll need to find some more."

Ferdie, Hedgehog and the doves
found Squirrel scampering after sunbeams.
"Snow is blowing in from the orchard," gasped Ferdie.
"It will be too cold for the butterflies, and the doves will
need to fly south, and poor Hedgehog must go back
to bed, and you must find some food."

"You're right. I've eaten my spring feast,"
said Squirrel, "all my stores are gone. But before
I hunt for more we need to tell the rabbits to
munch as much grass as they can
before the snow falls."

Ferdie, Squirrel, Hedgehog and the doves hurried off again.

The rabbits were playing roly-poly down the burrow-bank.
"Stop playing!" cried Ferdie. "There's snow blowing in
from the orchard. It will be too cold for the butterflies,
and the doves will need to fly south, and poor
Hedgehog must go back to bed, and Squirrel needs
to find food, and you must munch more grass."
"But before we eat," said the rabbits,
staggering dizzily to their feet…

…"Let's Go And
Play In The Snow!"

So the rabbits hoppity-roly-poly-plopped down the hill, through the wood. They were chased by the squirrel, the hedgehog, the doves, and a bouncy, full-of-importance fox, all the way to the orchard, where the ground was white with...

...BLOSSOM!

Blossom bobbing in the branches. Blossom blowing in the breeze.

Blossom blanketing the ground and not a snowflake to be found.

"That's blossom, not snow, you dotty fox!" the animals cried.

Ferdie blinked and rubbed his eyes, feeling very silly. But then…

. . . the animals scooped up paw and clawfuls of blossom
from the ground, and covered him in a tickly shower
of fluttering white petals! Ferdie dodged about
between the trees, showered from the sky and
every side, until at last they all collapsed
in a blossomy, soft white heap.

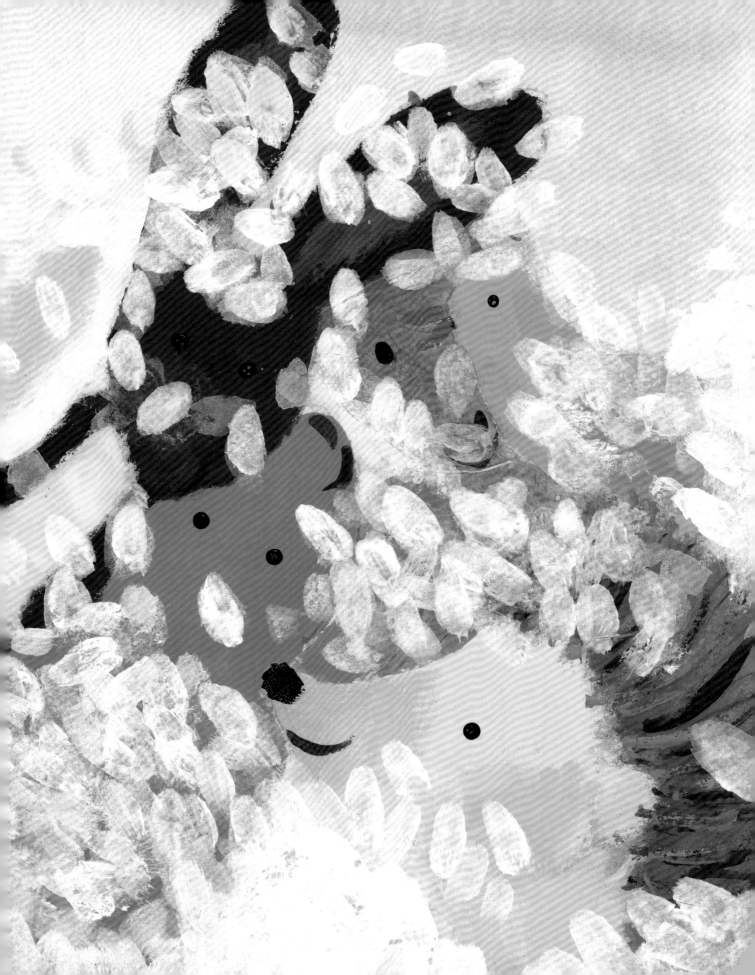

Then the doves
fluttered back to their
branch with beakfuls of
blossom to line their nest.

Hedgehog snuffled
off up the slope,
his prickles dotted
with tiny white petals.

Squirrel went chasing
up and down trees after
snow-white petals that
danced in the breeze,

and the rabbits
bounced back up
the hill, with blossom
to brighten their burrow.

But Ferdie just lay smiling in his
soft blossom bed, watching the frothy
blossom branches bobbing overhead.

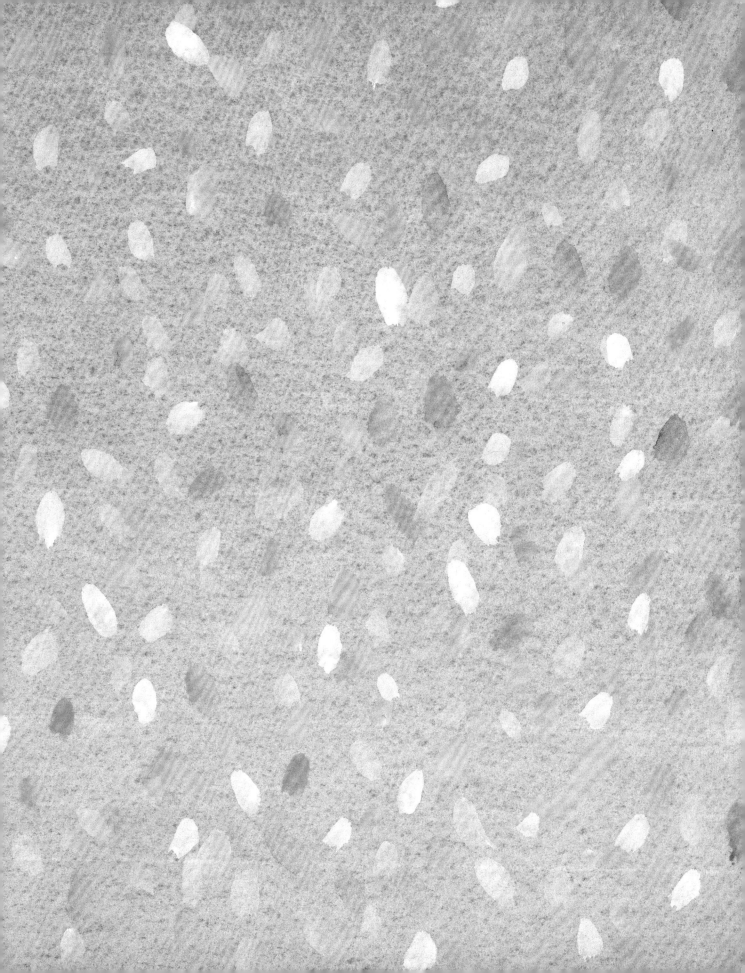

Other Tiphanie Beeke books for you to enjoy. . .

Ferdie and the Falling Leaves
written by Julia Rawlinson

Ferdie tries everything to stop the leaves falling from his tree.
But eventually the last one drops and the tree is bare – until the
next morning, when Ferdie gets a wonderful, wintry surprise!

From Me to You
written by Anthony France

Rat is fed up. He stays indoors. He doesn't see much of his friends –
until a mysterious letter arrives, telling Rat how special he is.
Did one of his friends send it? Off he goes to visit them all –
and remembers just how special *they* are!

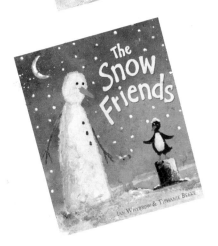

The Snow Friends
written by Ian Whybrow

Little Pig leads a quiet life – until he finds three new words
in his book: WISH, CHANGE, FRIEND. Putting the words
together, Little Pig sets out on a wonderful adventure,
leading to new discoveries and friendship. . .